BURP!

Hello?

How To Draw
Guapo

1.

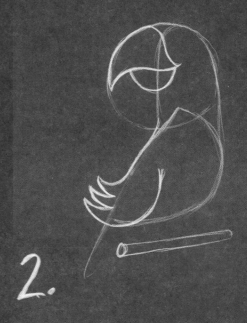

2.

3.

4.

5.

Would Someone Please Answer the Parrot!

Written by BERYL YOUNG   Illustrated by JASON DOLL

PEANUT BUTTER PRESS

To Neve and Misha—B.Y.

For Gabrielle—J.D.

Peanut Butter Press
9-1060 Dakota Street
Winnipeg, MB R2N 1P2
www.peanutbutterpress.ca

The artwork in this book was created using pen, ink and watercolour.

Book design by Lee Huscroft

Printed and bound in Hong Kong by Paramount Printing Company Limited/ Book Art Inc., Ontario, Canada

This book is Smyth sewn casebound.

5 4 3 2 1

LIBRARY AND ARCHIVES CANADA CATALOGUING IN PUBLICATION

Young, Beryl, 1934- author
    Would someone please answer the parrot! / written by Beryl Young; illustrated by Jason Doll.

ISBN 978-1-927735-00-8 (bound)

    I. Doll, Jason, 1970- illustrator II. Title.

PS8597.O575W68 2013   jC813'.6   C2013-902222-8

Uncle Bill arrived at the Gibson's door straight off the ship. He was carrying a cage that held a grey parrot with a bright red tail.

"Bought this fella from a breeder in Rotterdam. On the way back me mates taught Guapo a few words," said Uncle Bill.

"Gimme four!" Uncle Bill palmed Guapo's raised toes. Then he put Guapo back in the cage, ate a huge supper, burped loudly and left on the next ship for Zanzibar.

Guapo was the first pet the family ever had.
"Say something," said Zoe.
"Bombs away!" squawked Guapo, and he pooped on the floor of the cage.
Zoe and her twin brother Zack almost cracked up.
"Disgusting!" said Mom.
"I'm not cleaning up that mess," said Dad.
"Lemme outta here," screeched Guapo.
Dad said, "There's NO way that bird gets out of the cage."

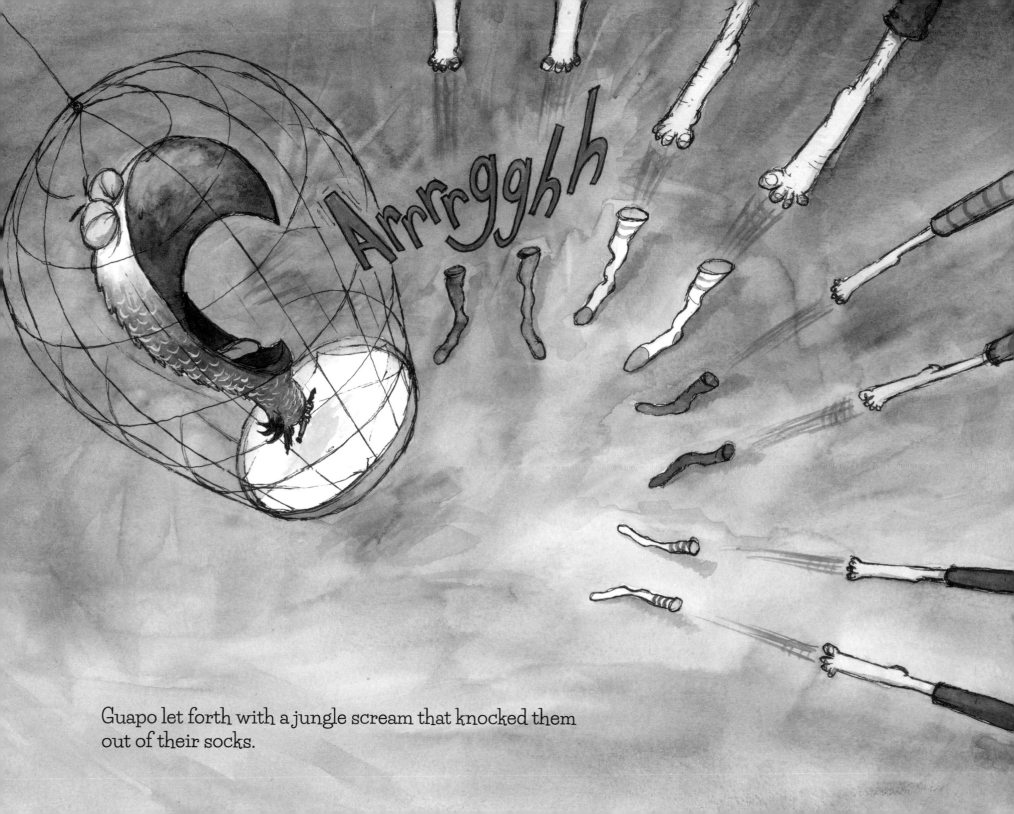

Guapo let forth with a jungle scream that knocked them out of their socks.

Guapo gave a piercing whistle. "Whilitt."

It was so loud it shattered the mirror over the fireplace.
"Stop that racket!" said Mom.

"Hi there, sweet stuff."

Guapo was excited and flapped his wings at Mom.

"I don't believe I heard that," Mom said.
Dad said, "This is too much."

"Too much. Too much," imitated Guapo.

Then he made his jungle scream again. "Arrrrgghh."
"That bird has to go," Dad said.
"Bye, big boy," Guapo screeched.

Then he burped just like Uncle Bill.

Burp!

The family soon learned that Guapo could imitate anything. First it was the phone.

Ringg Ringg

Two minutes later Guapo learned to imitate
the lawnmower down the street.

"Whhirrr-rr."

Three minutes later he learned to imitate car
alarms and fire sirens.
They had to bring Guapo inside.

"Guess what?" Dad said at the dinner table.
"Auntie Pattie's coming for her annual visit."

"Oh, no," moaned Zack. "She always brings me icky marzipan."
"She always brings me yucky hair elastics," said Zoe.
Mom said, "She can be a bit bossy at times."
"I know," groaned Dad, "and she stays waaay too long."

When Auntie Pattie arrived she gave Zack a marzipan bar and Zoe a bag of hair elastics.
"Aren't you going to thank me? I'd hoped you children had acquired more manners since last year.
Now go and wash your hands before lunch."

"Ringg . . . Ringg."
"Hurry up children. Get the phone!" ordered Auntie Pattie.

"It's just Guapo," the twins said together. "Come and meet him."
Guapo let out a wolf whistle. **"Hi there, sweet stuff!"**

Auntie Pattie threw up her hands.
"What an appalling creature!"

Guapo got so excited he made all his noises.
"What's the last one?" asked Zoe.
"The microwave," answered Zack.

That afternoon Zack fed the marzipan to Guapo, and Zoe hid the hair elastics under the paper at the bottom of his cage.

The next day when Auntie Pattie was having her toast and special oolong tea for breakfast, Guapo made the microwave beep sixteen times, the telephone ring thirteen times and followed up with eight big burps. Then he squawked quite clearly, "Bombs away!"

Auntie Pattie asked, "What's he saying that for?"
"You don't want to know," said Dad.
"More tea, Auntie Pattie?" said Zoe and Zack.

It looked like Auntie Pattie was settling in for another lengthy stay. She had put all her clothes in the dresser drawers and at night she hung her dripping panties over the bathroom shower rod. "That's gross," said Zack.

It wasn't long before Guapo was saying "Hiya Auntie Pantie" every time she came into the room. Finally Auntie Pattie had enough. "That's too much," she snapped.

"Too much. Too much. Too much," repeated Guapo.

Mom whispered, "Which one of you told Guapo about Auntie's panties?" The twins had been practising their innocent look.

That evening the door of Guapo's cage was left open. Guapo flew into the dining room and landed on Auntie Pattie's shoulder. He helped himself to a bite of the pork chop on her plate and tried to eat one of her ugly green earrings.

"For goodness sake, keep the door to Guapo's cage shut!" said Mom.
Dad shook his head. "That bird HAS to go. He's just too much."
"Just too much . . . just too . . ."
"OH, BE QUIET!" shrieked Auntie Pattie.
"OH, BEQUIET! BEQUIET!" Gaupo shrieked back.
"DO something!" demanded Auntie Pattie.
"Like what?" Mom and Dad said together.

The next day Guapo was screeching along to the children's rap music. Auntie Pattie escaped to the front porch for some peace and quiet, but instead found herself listening to the barking of the dog next door and the whining of the lawnmower down the street. The telephone rang.

"Rringg . . . Rringg!"

Auntie Pattie waited. "Rringg!" The dog kept barking and a police siren sounded a few blocks away . . . and the telephone kept ringing.

In exasperation she yelled,
"Would someone please
answer the parrot!"
Then she looked horrified
and Dad heard her mutter,
"I must be losing my mind."

That night Auntie Pattie was exhausted and went to bed early. In the middle of her dreams she heard a voice from the end of the bed. "Hi there, sweet stuff!"

Auntie Pattie sat up straight. It sounded like a man in the room. Something brushed past her and landed on the bedpost.

Auntie Pattie screamed.
Guapo screamed.
Everyone came running.
"Who let that parrot out of the cage?" asked Mom.
"Stop laughing all of you," she said to her family.

Bombs away!

The next morning Auntie came out of the bedroom with her suitcases. "I'm leaving," she announced.
"Will you be coming back next year?" asked Zoe and Zach politely.
"I'm not coming back until you get rid of that bird!" she snarled.

"Auntie Pantie pants on fire!"
screeched Guapo as Auntie Pattie drove away in a taxi.

"Well, kids, I guess we've got ourselves a pet," Dad said.
"Yaaay!" cheered Zack and Zoe.   "Gimme four!" squawked Guapo.

A Word About African Grey Parrots:

African Grey Parrots come from the tropical forests of Africa and are a threatened species due to destruction of their habitat and their capture for the pet trade. According to international treaties governing the trade in wildlife, parrots can still be legally captured in the wild and sold in three African countries, though they remain protected in several more. Captive-raised parrots can be purchased, but proper documentation is needed if you transport a parrot from one country to another.

African Greys are said to be the most intelligent birds in the world. They are very social and love to interact with humans.

African Grey Parrots have light grey feathers and bright red tails. White feathers form a mask over the parrot's large yellow eyes. These birds can grow as tall as 35 centimetres and weigh about 400 grams. They can live to be 60 years old.

In the wild the diet of African Greys includes fruit, berries, seeds, nuts and vegetation. As pets they can be fed grains (in the form of pellets) and many kinds of human foods such as fruit (especially grapes and apples, but not avocados), vegetables, nuts and small amounts of cooked meat.

African Greys are capable of a remarkable range of imitations. They can mimic human speech, all kinds of animal sounds and machines–even those that emit electronic noises, including video games. Some members of this species have been known to acquire a vocabulary of over 900 words and demonstrate the ability to combine words in inventive ways. An example of this is the parrot who says "long yellow" when he wants a cob of corn.

For more information about African Greys and efforts to save them, please visit:
www.parrots.org/flyfree/

*Guapo is a Congo African Grey Parrot, but there is a second subspecies–the Timneh African Grey–that is also a popular pet and can imitate speech and sounds.

**Parrots would probably enjoy the taste of marzipan because it's made of crushed almonds, egg whites and sugar, but should not be fed this sweet treat, especially if it's covered with chocolate. It's not wise to let parrots, or any pets, eat chocolate.

I would like to thank my great friend Roberta Rich who introduced me to Guapo. I didn't know much about parrots, but I knew a smart bird when I saw one. So one summer afternoon, with lots of help from Roberta (and her homemade grape wine), this story was born. Thanks to Bruce Carscadden for the title.

I would also like to thank my pals who read the manuscript: Debbie Hodge, Norma Charles, Linda Bailey, Deanne Young, Susan Moger, Shelley Hrdlitschka and Dianne Woodman, along with Carol Szuminsky of Peanut Butter Press, such an easy editor to work with. Special thanks to Jason Doll, whose brilliant illustrations add so much to Guapo's story, and to Lee Huscroft for his imaginative design concept.

—*Beryl Young*